Blue Mouse
World
is
Different Now
BY DREW ABBOT

My sister and brother told me to come, and my friend Walt because I need your help! I'm engaged to my fiancé Grace but I have feel something with this other girl, she doesn't have a name (since her parents ran out of the hospital after one second after she was born) but even though I don't have a name to call her I still feel something with her, so, who do I choose?
Inside the tent
In the most intense situations you reveal who you really are and what you really care about, let me show you the future

WOOOOOSH!
The flames roared as the vision began!!!!

Blue Mouse world was the place everyone wanted to go

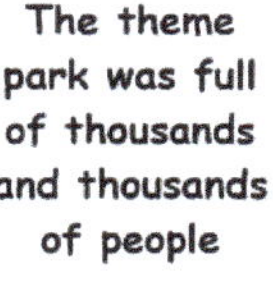

The theme
park was full
of thousands
and thousands
of people

The vision was showing the future of Wutus, a blonde girl called Grace and a brunette who's parents never named so she went through life with no name (Or did she?)

Grace wasn't happy seeing him kiss another woman

He gave an awkward look because it was at this point he knew he had messed up

Detective Shanara: Wutus! We're secret F.I.B government agents and this is gonna be alot to take in but
Detective Sapphire: Look Blue Mouse have the abilities to take over the minds of every meat eater in the park. Somehow you're the only vegetarian here so we need you to

This is not a funny prank
Get the hell away from me
Get the hell away from me before I call the actual cops.

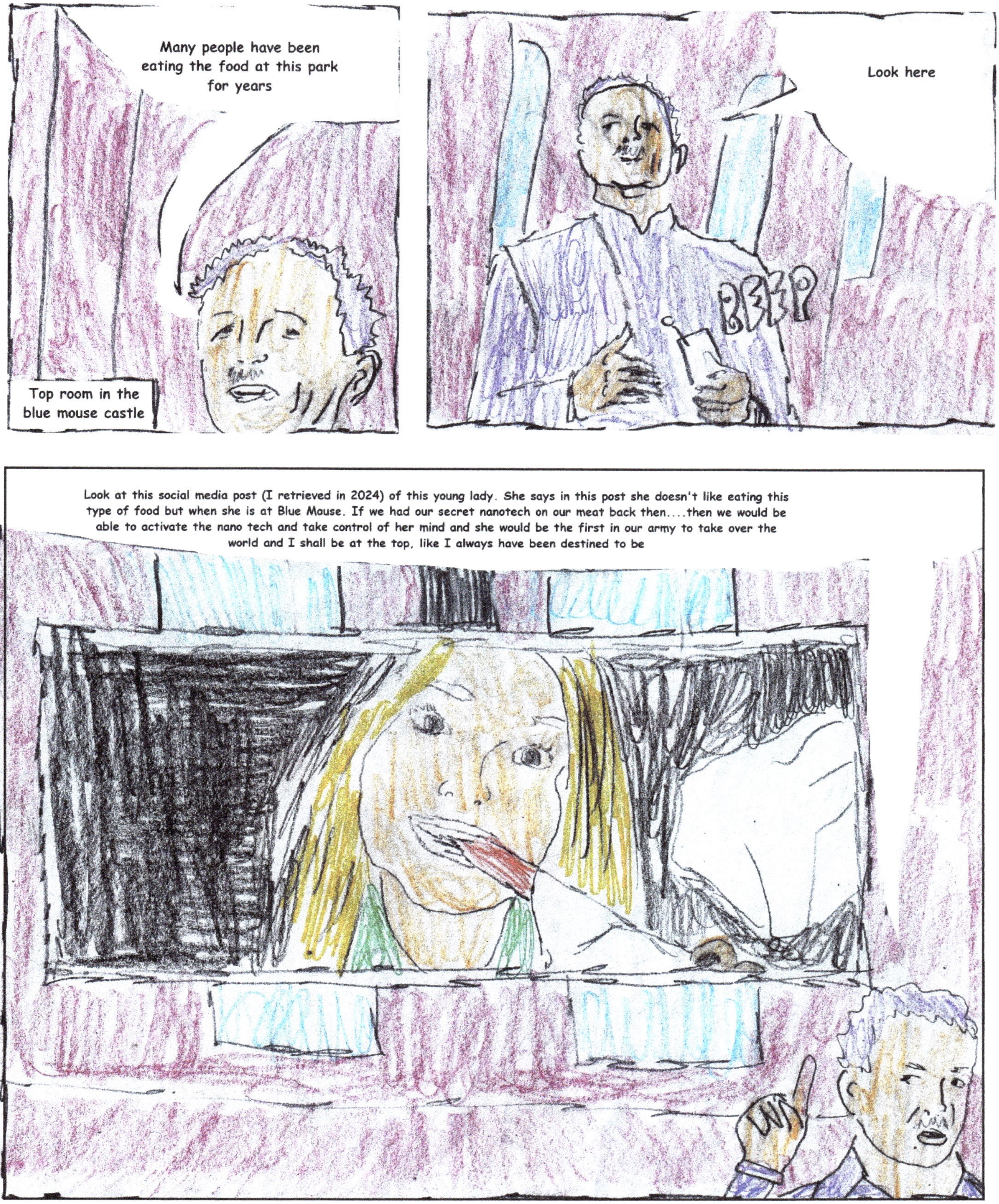

Look at this social media post (I retrieved in 2024) of this young lady. She says in this post she doesn't like eating this type of food but when she is at Blue Mouse. If we had our secret nanotech on our meat back then....then we would be able to activate the nano tech and take control of her mind and she would be the first in our army to take over the world and I shall be at the top, like I always have been destined to be

11 years ago in 2015 Every single member of staff that worked on Blue Mouse Channel (Even the stars) had technology that could turn themselves invisible and had a secret hideout but the secret division fell apart when everyone realized how weird it was

I don't even
love Grace....

I'm in love
with somebody
else

Congrats you've won a free stay in the castle sweet. The staff will have all your luggage sent directly there.
WOW NO WAY!
EEEEEEEEEEE!
EEEEEE EEEEEE EEEEEE EEEEEE EEEEEE EEEEEE EEEEEK
NO WAY!
Bsst, please we're trying to help you. Don't go up there it's a trap just come with us and we can get you to sa-
GET OUT OF OUR WAY!
Well it's your funeral dude

Helloooo Wutus, Grace...and...um...girl in red...You are forcefully invited to be the very first to have their digested nanobots (On the blue mouse world meat) to tickle you inside your stomachs and tickle you and tickle you into insanity so that your mind becomes lost and we take your mind and create an army, an army to take over the world. But don't worry this will be beautiful and you will smile.
Isn't that fantastic heh heh heh
What can be better than dying with a smile on your face?

You are happy.....RIGHT!?

The three had no idea how to react

Oh my gosh we're surrounded by invisible people!? FIGHT!
POW!
Invisible Grunts: Ow!

AAAAAAAHHHHH!!!!
Invisible agents: Stop them! They're heading towards the balcony!

Balconey
There's no where to go!
No name you were the one that I loved!
You it was....you
Grace:
Well
thanks alot
My name is Joeline

BEEP!

Won't work, I'm a vegetarian....oh wait is that a gun?
PAHAHAHAHA HAHAHAHAHA HAHAHA! NO! NO! PAHAAAAAAH AHAHAHAHAHA!!!!
THUD!
NO PAHAHAHAHA! M-MAKE IT PAHAHAHAHAHAHA MAKE IT STOP! PAHAHAHAHAHAHA HAHA
THUDE

GASP!

In the heat of the moment what did you learn?

Well, I learnt I'm not going to Blue Mouse World next year